The Creek Nation

by Allison Lassieur

Consultant:
Edwin Marshall
Program Administrator
Muscogee (Creek) Nation

Bridgestone Books
an imprint of Capstone Press
Mankato, Minnesota

Bridgestone Books are published by Capstone Press
151 Good Counsel Drive, P.O. Box 669, Mankato, Minnesota 56002
http://www.capstone-press.com

Library of Congress Cataloging-in-Publication Data
Lassieur, Allison.
    The Creek Nation/by Allison Lassieur.
    p. cm.—(Native peoples)
    Includes bibliographical references and index.
    ISBN 0-7368-0947-3
    1. Creek Indians—Juvenile literature. [1. Creek Indians. 2. Indians of North America.] I. Title.
II. Series.
E99.C9 L37 2002
975.004'973—dc21
                                                          00-012596

Summary: An overview of the Creek Nation, including a description of their homes, food,
clothing, history, government, religion, towns, and the Creek Confederacy.

Editorial Credits
Rebecca Glaser, editor; Karen Risch, product planning editor; Timothy Halldin, cover designer;
    Heidi Meyer, illustrator; Jeff Anderson, photo researcher

Photo Credits
Archive Photos, 20
Eastern National, 6
Edwin Marshall, 8
Jack Boedecker, 16, 18
Karen Gibson, 10, 14
Perry Berryhill, cover
Phyllis Fife, 12

1 2 3 4 5 6 07 06 05 04 03 02

Table of Contents

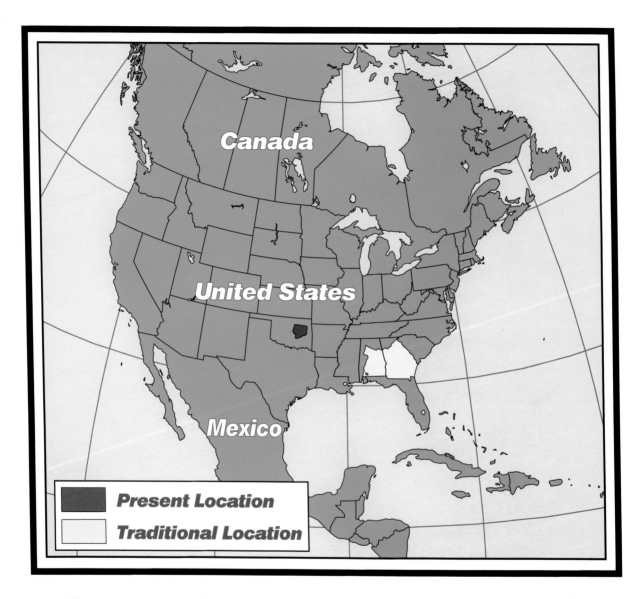

Present Location

Traditional Location

Years ago, the Creek people lived in the area that is now Alabama and Georgia. Today, most Creeks live in Oklahoma. A small number of Creeks still live in Alabama.

Fast Facts

Today, most Creek people live like other North Americans. But they continue some of their traditions and are proud of their history. These facts tell about the Creeks' past.

Name: The Creek people call themselves Muscogee. Europeans called the Muscogee "Creek" because they lived near creeks and rivers. Their official name today is the Muscogee (Creek) Nation.

Homes: Creek families had a summer house and a winter house. Summer houses did not have any walls. They were open and cool. Winter houses had walls. They kept people warm in cold weather.

Food: The Creeks were farmers. Women planted corn, beans, squash, and other crops. They also picked wild berries, fruits, plants, and nuts. Men hunted animals such as deer and wild boar. They also hunted rabbits, ducks, geese, and other small animals. Creek men also fished in rivers.

Clothing: Creek men wore breechcloths made of deerskin or cloth. Women dressed in skirts made of grass or deerskin. Both men and women wrapped woven grass blankets around their shoulders in winter.

Language: The Creek language is a Muscogean language. Many American Indians in the southeastern United States spoke Muscogean languages.

Creek History

Many Creek groups lived in the southeastern United States. In 1540, a Spanish explorer named Hernando de Soto met the Creeks. Later, other settlers moved there and traded with the Creeks.

Some Creeks fought with Great Britain against the colonies during the Revolutionary War (1775–1783). The colonies won the war. The new U.S. government took more of the Creeks' land. Many Creeks adopted the early settlers' European culture. Other Creeks wanted to keep their traditions.

Two Creek groups fought against each other in the Creek Wars (1813–1814). The U.S. government took more Creek land when the war was over.

In 1836, the U.S. government forced the Creeks to move to Indian Territory. This journey now is called the Trail of Tears. Many Creeks died during this long march. Some Creeks hid in the forests of Georgia and Florida. Today, the descendants of those people are members of the Seminole tribe.

The Battle of Horseshoe Bend ended the Creek War. Today, the battle site is a national park in Alabama.

Homes, Food, and Clothing

Creek families had summer and winter houses. The summer house was a platform with four poles and a thatched roof. Winter houses were warm. The Creeks wove tree branches between large posts to make the walls. They put a clay and grass mixture over the branches. They made the roof from tree bark.

Corn was the Creeks' most important crop. Women took care of the corn fields. They also gathered berries, nuts, fruits, and plants. Men hunted deer. They used traps, spears, and nets to fish. They also fished by putting a plant called devil's shoestring in a river. The plant was safe for people, but it killed the fish. The men collected the dead fish as they floated to the surface.

The Creeks dressed in lightweight clothing in the warm southeastern weather. Men wore a piece of deerskin called a breechcloth that hung from the waist. Women made skirts from deerskin, grass, or tree bark.

The Creek wore clothes made of cloth after they began trading with Europeans.

Creek Families

Long ago, Creek families were part of large groups of relatives called clans. Each clan was named after an animal. Every town had members from each clan.

Every person in a clan was related through the mother's side of the family. Members of the mother's family cared for the children. Aunts taught girls how to cook and how to make pottery. Uncles showed boys how to hunt.

Creek people had to marry someone from a different clan. A man asked the members of a woman's clan if he could marry her. The man and woman had to show that they would be good partners. The man built a house for the woman. The woman cooked food for the man. The marriage was final after the couple finished these tasks.

Today, many generations of a Creek family live together. A firstborn child often is raised by its grandparents. They teach the child about Creek values and beliefs.

Creek grandparents help raise their grandchildren.

How the Clans Came to Be

This Creek story tells how the clans were created. In the beginning, the Creek people crawled out of a hole in the ground. At first, all Creek people lived together. The Creator then sent a thick fog to cover the world. The people could not see. They wandered into small groups. The small groups stayed together. They were afraid of being alone.

The Creator felt sorry for the people. He blew the fog away. The people sang songs of happiness. The members of the groups stayed together. They promised to treat each other like family.

Each group gave itself a name. One group honored the wind that had blown the fog away. They called themselves the Wind Clan. Other groups chose the name of the first animal they saw when the fog went away.

The Creator said to the groups, "You are the beginning of your clans. Live up to your name. Muscogeans will always be powerful."

Artist Phyllis Fife painted this picture that shows how animals appeared to the clans.

This is one of four tree shelters that stands on the ceremonial grounds where the Green Corn Ceremony takes place. Each of these arbors stands for one direction—north, south, east, or west.

Creek Beliefs

The Creeks are very spiritual people. Religion is important in everyday life. Some Creeks follow other religions such as Christianity. Most Creeks also have traditional beliefs. Plants, animals, fire, and water are part of these beliefs.

The Green Corn Ceremony is the most important Creek celebration. It is the beginning of the New Year for the Creeks. The Creek name for this ceremony is "Poskita Thokko." It is held during the ripening of the new corn crop.

The Creeks celebrate the Green Corn Ceremony at several ceremonial grounds. The ceremony lasts four to seven days during the summer. The Creeks tell stories, forgive others, and renew friendships at this time. They celebrate by dancing and singing around a fire. The smoke from the fire carries their praises to the Creator.

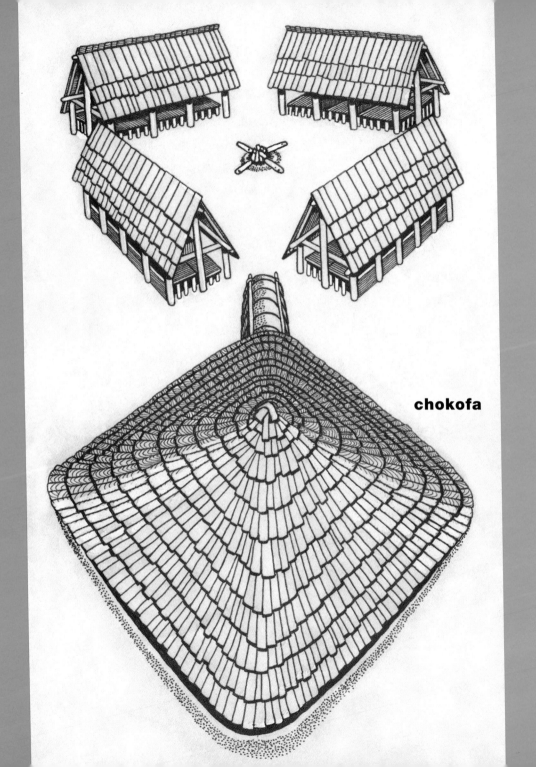

chokofa

Creek Towns

The town was the center of Creek life. The Creeks built their towns near creeks or rivers. These towns were called italwas. Creeks could easily find wood, animals to hunt, and good soil near the creeks.

Most towns had a council house called a chokofa. Councils met in these large, cone-shaped buildings during winter. Some chokofas held up to 500 people. In the summer, councils met outdoors. People watched meetings and ceremonies from four buildings that faced an open square.

A large playing field was near the chokofa and square. The Creeks used it for ceremonies and games. They played a game called stickball. Town leaders watched the games from long rows of seats that faced the field.

Creek families built their homes around the middle of town. Each family had storage buildings and small gardens. The whole tribe planted crops in a large, shared field outside the town.

A sacred fire was lit in the middle of each town square. The chokofa was near the square.

The Creek Confederacy

About 300 years ago, the Creek Nation had more than 50 towns. Some towns had only a few members. Other towns held hundreds of people. All the towns formed a group called a confederacy.

Each town in the confederacy had its own chief, called a mekko. The mekkos sometimes held council meetings to talk about problems facing all Creeks.

Creek towns in the confederacy were identified as red or white. Red towns were war towns. White towns were peace towns. When the Creeks went to war, the council chose a war chief from a red town. Peace talks always took place in a white town after a war.

When the Creeks won a war, the council invited the loser to join the confederacy. Many towns agreed. The confederacy grew larger and stronger. The Creek Confederacy became the most powerful tribe in the southeastern United States.

Mekkos from different towns met in the chokofa during winter.

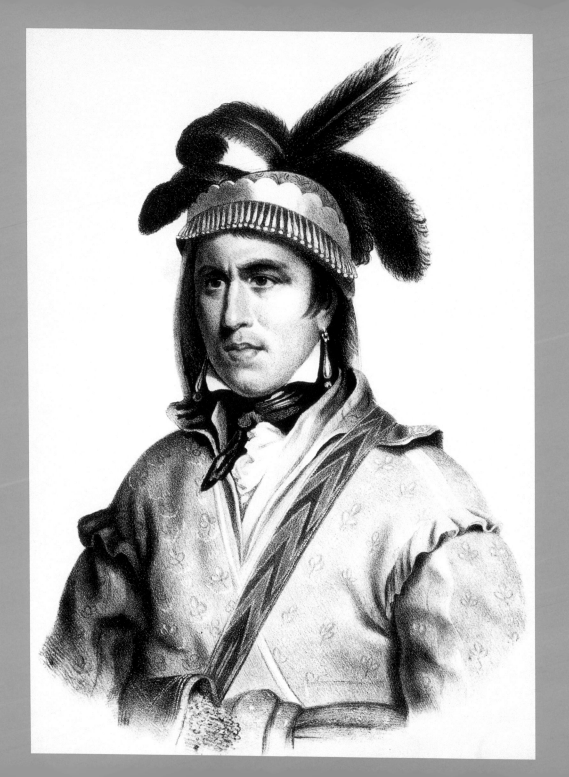

Creek Government

Long ago, the Creek did not have one leader. Each town thought of itself as a separate group. A town had many leaders. The Creek chose people who were honest and strong to be their leaders. Those leaders picked a mekko. The mekko was in charge of the well-being of the tribe.

The mekko also was part of the Creek council. The council was made up of mekkos from all the Creek towns. The council met to talk about planting, hunting, war, and other issues.

Today, the Creek Nation has a three-part government. The National Council has 26 members. The council makes laws for the tribe. The Creeks elect a principal chief and a second chief. They have jobs similar to the president and vice president of the United States. Six judges are appointed to the Supreme Court. They decide cases about tribal laws.

Opoethle Yahola was a Creek mekko during the early 1800s. He tried to keep the U.S. government from taking Creek lands.

Hands On: Make Grape Dumplings

The Creeks ate many wild fruits. Creek women made a special dessert from opossum grapes called grape dumplings. This modern version of the recipe uses grape juice instead of opossum grapes. Ask an adult to help you use the stove.

What You Need

Measuring cups and spoons
1 cup (250 mL) flour
1/2 teaspoon (2 mL) salt
2 1/2 cups (625 mL) grape juice
Medium bowl

Saucepan
1/4 cup (50 mL) sugar
Wooden spoon
Knife
Kitchen timer

What You Do

1. Pour flour, salt, and 1/2 cup (125 mL) grape juice in a bowl. Mix with wooden spoon to make dough.
2. Put 2 cups (500 mL) grape juice and sugar in a saucepan. Warm it on the stove until the sugar dissolves. Let the mixture cook on low heat while you do step 3.
3. Cut small pieces of dough and flatten them. Carefully place the dough pieces into the simmering grape juice and sugar mixture. Let the dumplings cook for 10-12 minutes.
4. Dumplings can be served either hot or cold.

Words to Know

breechcloth (BREECH-kloth)—a piece of deerskin clothing that hangs from the waist

ceremony (SER-uh-moh-nee)—formal actions, words, or music that honor a person, an event, or a higher being

Christianity (krist-chee-AN-uh-tee)—a religion based on the life and teachings of Jesus Christ

colony (KOL-uh-nee)—an area where people from another country have settled; the American colonies fought for independence from Great Britain during the Revolutionary War.

confederacy (kuhn-FED-ur-uh-see)—a union of towns or tribes with a common goal

council (KOUN-suhl)—a group of leaders

Indian Territory (IN-dee-uhn TER-uh-tor-ee)—land in what is now Oklahoma; the U.S. government forced many American Indians to move to Indian Territory in the 1800s.

thatch (THATCH)—a roofing made of straw, leaves, or grasses

Read More

Ansary, Mir Tamim. *Southeast Indians.* Native Americans. Des Plaines, Ill.: Heinemann Library, 2000.

Bruchac, Joseph. *The Great Ball Game: A Muskogee Story.* New York: Dial Books for Young Readers, 1994.

Newman, Shirlee P. *The Creek.* A First Book. New York: Franklin Watts, 1996.

Useful Addresses

Horseshoe Bend National Military Park
11288 Horseshoe Bend Road
Daviston, AL 36256

Muscogee (Creek) Nation
P.O. Box 580
Okmulgee, OK 74447

Internet Sites

Creek Nation
http://www.tourokmulgee.com/creek.html
Muscogee (Creek) Nation of Oklahoma
http://www.ocevnet.org/creek/index.html
North Georgia Creek History
http://www.georgiajournal.com/history/creekhistory.html

Index